Who Broke the Vase?

Written and illustrated by
Jeffrey Turner

Aladdin
NEW YORK LONDON TORONTO
SYDNEY NEW DELHI

For Ben, Colin, and Charlie.
Being truthful is better than being perfect.

ALADDIN / An imprint of Simon & Schuster Children's Publishing Division / 1230 Avenue of the Americas, New York, New York 10020 / First Aladdin hardcover edition April 2017 / Copyright © 2017 by Jeffrey Turner / All rights reserved, including the right of reproduction in whole or in part in any form. / ALADDIN is a trademark of Simon & Schuster, Inc. and related logo is a registered trademark of Simon & Schuster, Inc. / For information about special discounts for bulk purchases, please contact Simon & Schuster Special Sales at 1-866-506-1949 or business@simonandschuster.com. / The Simon & Schuster Speakers Bureau can bring authors to your live event. For more information or to book an event contact the Simon & Schuster Speakers Bureau at 1-866-248-3049 or visit our website at www.simonspeakers.com. / Book designed by Karin Paprocki / The illustrations for this book were rendered digitally. / The text of this book was set in Nanami HM Book. / Manufactured in China 0117 SCP / 2 4 6 8 10 9 7 5 3 1 / Library of Congress Control Number 2016936748 / ISBN 978-1-4814-7953-0 (hc) / ISBN 978-1-4814-7954-7 (eBook)

An elephant walked through the room and accidentally bumped into the vase with his trunk.

Did I say an elephant?
I meant a mouse.
A mouse was inside the
vase and knocked it over
trying to get out.

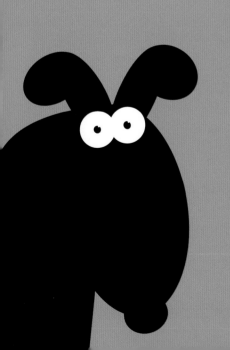

Oh, wait!

It wasn't a mouse.
A crow flew in through
the window and
landed on the vase
and knocked it over.
Yes, a crow.

Ummmm. It was a sheep. He was showing me how to knit wool mittens, and his leg accidentally knocked over the vase.

Maybe, just maybe, it wasn't a sheep. Now I remember. A baby did it, but I am sure she didn't mean to break the vase.

You sure?

Then it MUST have been the hippo that I saw in the living room. They are very large, you know, and he probably bumped into the vase by accident.

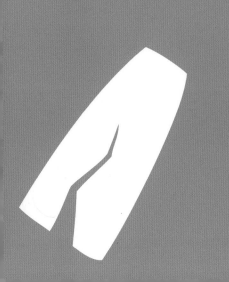

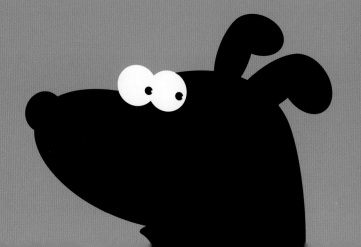

Yes, I broke the vase.

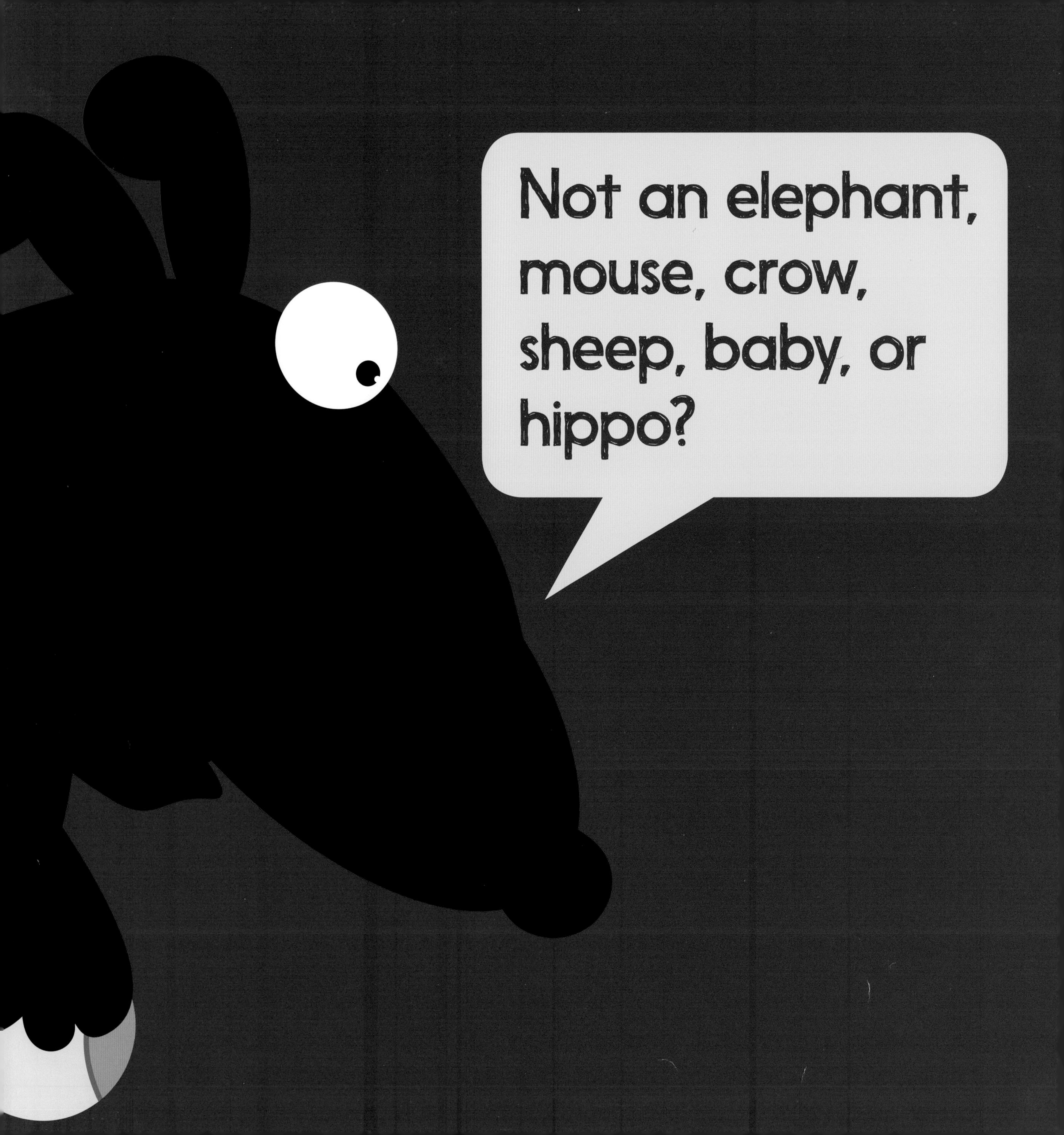
Not an elephant, mouse, crow, sheep, baby, or hippo?

Of course not!
I mean, who would
believe that?

Can we go out
and play now?

A huge grasshopper was playing leapfrog with his friends when he jumped too high...